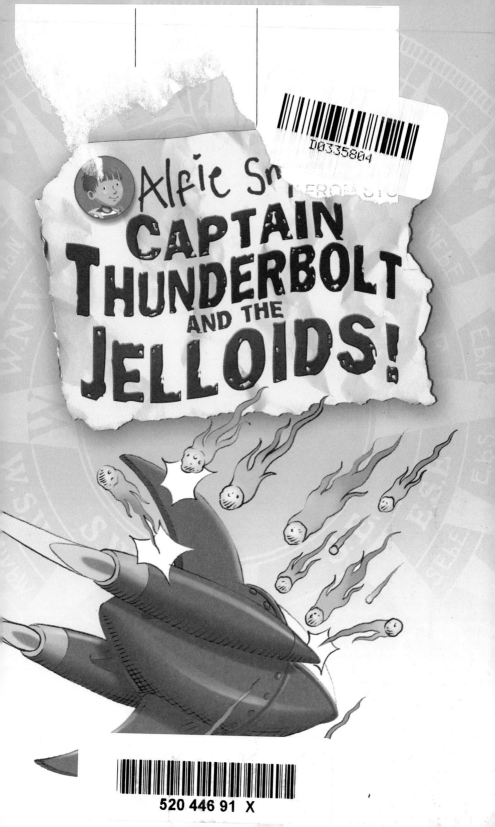

Alfie Sm...

CAPTAIN THUNDERBOLT
AND THE
JELLOIDS!

Mum,
I have gone exploring.
Got my rucksack. Don't
worry, I'll be home in
time for tea. Love, Alfie X

Here's the note I always
leave for Mum before I go
on another adventure

ALFIE SMALL JOURNAL 4: Captain Thunderbolt and the Jelloids
A DAVID FICKLING BOOK 978 1 849 92122 0

Published in Great Britain by David Fickling Books,
a division of Random House Publishers UK
A Random House Group Company

This edition published 2013

1 3 5 7 9 10 8 6 4 2

DAVID FICKLING BOOKS
31 Beaumont Street, Oxford, OX1 2NP

www.kidsatrandomhouse.co.uk
www.totallyrandombooks.co.uk
www.randomhouse.co.uk

Addresses for companies within The Random House Group Limited can be found at:
www.randomhouse.co.uk/offices.htm

THE RANDOM HOUSE GROUP Limited Reg. No. 954009

A CIP catalogue record for this book is available from the British Library.

Printed in China

Photographs of Alfie's finds by Ian Rycroft. www.ianrycroft.co.uk

This is the Adventure Journal of

Alfie Small

Hobbies: Exploring and having adventures!

My best friend: Jed

Things I Like: Bopple and

Captain Thunderbolt

Things I Hate:

Jelloids and gunge!

1. Take-Off!

This is me →

Jed →

↑ This is my explorer's kit

My name is Alfie Small, and this is my best friend, Jed. I'm a famous explorer and have lots of dangerous adventures. I always take my rucksack of useful things with me, just in case!

At the bottom of my garden, behind the rickety shed, is the special place I go exploring. The grass is long and the weeds grow thick, and I never know what I might find.

Today, I pushed through the weeds . . . and found a squat little rocket pointing towards the sky. It had two powerful engines and long, curved fins like a shark.

Stabilising fin

"Oh, brilliant! Come on, Jed," I cried, clambering aboard. Jed jumped up beside me.

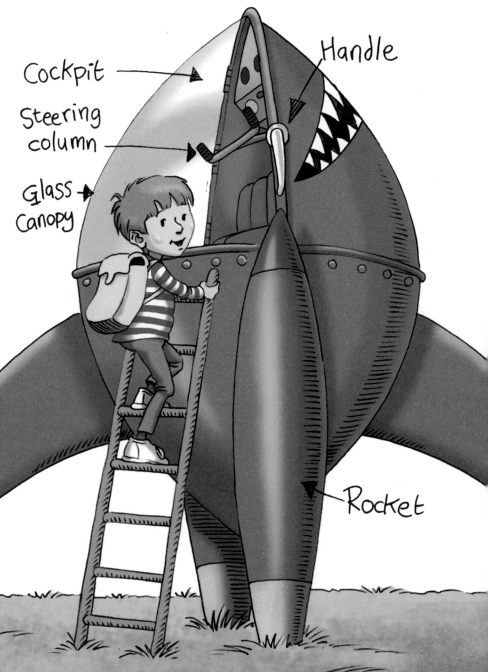

Cockpit

Steering column

Glass Canopy

Handle

Rocket

I pushed a button, pulled a lever
and *Whoosh!* The engines roared
like dragons, sending out tongues of
flame and clouds of billowing smoke.
Shuddering and shaking, the rocket
rose above the trees and ripped through
the clouds. Up and up and up, it went,
higher and higher.

We roared right up into the blackness of space. Jed stared out of the window, his tail wagging with excitement.

"Wow! It's so quiet up here," I said. But I had spoken too soon.

Rat-a-tat-tat! Giant hailstones started bashing against our rocket ship.

"Oh, yikes!" I cried. "Hold on, Jed!" We had flown right into a shower of red-hot meteors!

Our rocket went spinning round and round. Soon we couldn't tell which way was home.

Battered and dented but still in one piece, our tough little rocket ship passed through the fiery downpour. We drifted amongst shimmering stars and silent planets that glowed like coloured lanterns.

All at once – *Fizzle! Hiss! Bzzz* – the rocket ship's radio sputtered into life.

"Mayday! Mayday!" said a tinny, crackly voice. "Please help us!"

MAYDAY!

2. Alien Attack!

"Who are you? State your position," I shouted into the ship's microphone, my heart pounding with excitement.

"My name is Bopple, and I'm from the planet Burble," crackled the voice. "Our Queen has been taken prisoner. Please help!"

I looked out of the window at all the spinning worlds. "But which planet is yours?" I asked.

"It's the orange one, but watch out for the horrible–" *Fizzle! Pop!* Suddenly the voice cut out.

"Hello? Come in, Bopple. Come in!" I cried, but there was no answer. "Let's go, Jed. Bopple needs us!" I said. But Jed wasn't listening. He was growling at something. I followed his gaze out of the cockpit.

"Uh-oh! This looks like trouble."

A pack of green, walrus-shaped space creatures were heading straight for us. They flew along at great speed, using their propeller-like tails. They each had one beady eye and a wide drooling mouth, and their bodies were as shiny and wobbly as jelly.

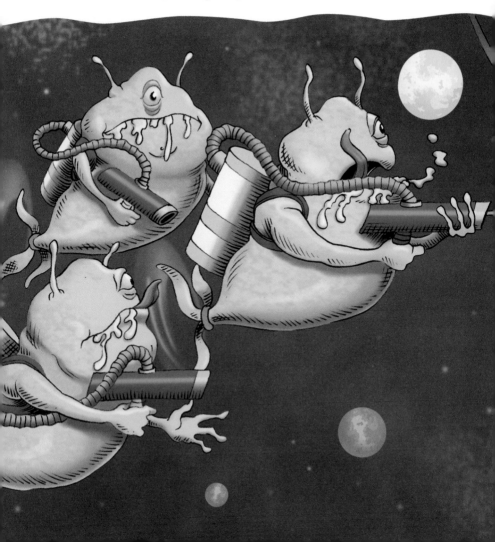

As they drew near, the creatures aimed strange, cylindrical gadgets at us. *Boosh!* Jets of gunge shot from them, and *Kersplat!* they splattered against our rocket, making it judder and sway. I yanked the control column and sent us zigzagging away.

With their propeller tails whining, the grinning monsters gave chase.

"DON'T FIRE!" I bellowed into the microphone, but the brutes ignored me.

Splat! Thick gunk hit one of our engines and clogged up its pipes. It spluttered and died, and our little rocket began to fall.

"Brace yourself, Jed," I shouted. "We're going to crash!"

3. A Helping Hand

Splash! By a strange fluke our rocket landed slap bang in the middle of a massive lake on the Burbles' orange planet. We skidded across its surface like a pebble and juddered to a halt. I opened the cockpit.

"We'll have to swim for it, Jed," I said, stepping out onto the rocket's hull. But when I dipped a foot into the lake, the liquid clung to my shoe like treacle. "More gunk! It's much too thick to swim in."

With a terrible gurgle, our rocket
began to sink into the syrupy gunge.

"What are we going to do?" I cried,
desperately rummaging in my rucksack
for anything that might help. String,
maps, pencils and glue – they were no
good. Oh yikes! Another minute and
we would disappear below the surface
for ever.

Buzz! A faint humming noise filled the air, and scudding over the lake came an open-topped flying saucer, driven by a man in a space suit. He brought his flying saucer to a stop and hovered above us.

"Quick, climb aboard,"
he bellowed, reaching
down with a gloved
hand.

I hesitated.
Was this spaceman
friendly?

"Jump to it, lad," he ordered. "The
Jelloids are coming and they've got
gungerators!"

Zooming over the water was a gang of the same green space gangsters that had splattered my rocket.

"Oh, yikes!" I hollered, grabbing the spaceman's hand. He pulled Jed and me onto his flying saucer.

Zap! A jet of gunge whizzed past my ear.

"Woof, woof!" barked Jed, as our spaceman friend put his flying saucer into super-drive and we shot away with the Jelloids in hot pursuit.

ZAP!

ZAP!

4. Captain Ace Thunderbolt

"**I**'m Alfie Small, famous explorer," I yelled above the whine of the engine. "Who are you?"

"Captain Ace Thunderbolt of Space Patrol, scourge of alien baddies everywhere. We picked up a Mayday call from the Burbles."

"Me too," I cried.

"Looks like they've been invaded by Jelloids," said the Captain, as we whizzed across the barren terrain.

"Why?" I asked. "There's nothing here but lakes of gunge!"

"Don't ask me, but I've dealt with Jelloids before, and they're a nasty bunch," bawled the Captain.

Zap! Another jet of gunge just missed us.

"They're getting closer," I warned him.

"Leave them to me," said Captain Thunderbolt. "You keep an eye out for the Burbles."

"What do they look like?" I asked.

"No idea!" said the Captain.

Jelloids began to appear on all sides. Soon we were surrounded!

"Have no fear, Alfie," said Thunderbolt as the aliens took aim with their gungerators. "I can easily dodge this lot."

Kersplat! Kersplodge! The Captain was instantly covered in gunge.

"Jumping Jupiter! I can't see a thing – take over, Alfie Small!"

I grabbed the controls as the Jelloids closed in on us. I didn't know which way to turn. Then I saw a massive crater up ahead and steered right for it!

5. Escape Into Darkness

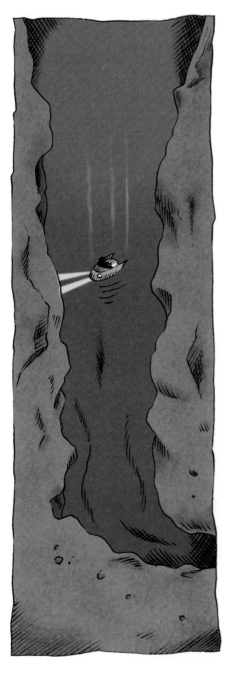

Whoosh! We flew into the crater and dropped like a supersonic lift, deeper and deeper into the core of the planet.

"Orbiting aliens! Where are we?" cried Thunderbolt. We were speeding along a dark, narrow tunnel at two hundred miles an hour.

"Lost!" I said, wrenching the steering wheel this

way and that. "But we've shaken off the Jelloids!"

"Then slow down, PLEASE!" spluttered the Captain, wiping the gunk from his visor.

"Where's the brake?" I cried as we scraped against the rocky wall and sent a shower of sparks cascading behind us. The Captain yanked a lever on the dashboard and the flying saucer slowed down.

Up ahead, the narrow tunnel opened out into a wide, dim cavern. As we flew in, a crowd of the strangest little aliens dived behind tall stalagmites that grew from the ground like crooked fingers. I pulled the brake lever and our flying saucer slowed to a stop, nestling gently on the ground.

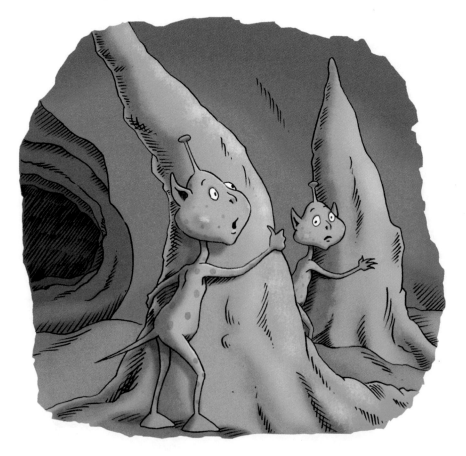

Captain Thunderbolt leaped out
and ducked behind the saucer. "These
subterranean aliens might be dangerous.
Let's wait for them to make their move,"
he whispered.

We waited, and waited, but nothing
happened. All of a sudden, I realized
that Jed was missing.

"Jed, where are you?" I yelled, and
heard his familiar bark coming from
amongst the stalagmites.

"They've got him!" exclaimed
Thunderbolt. "The fiends!"

"Oh, no!" I cried, but then Jed trotted round the side of the saucer, with a daft grin on his face. With him was one of the aliens, his own little space dog scuttling along beside him.

"Here you are, at last, " said the space creature in a buzzy, humming voice. "I'm Bopple. Come on, we don't have much time!"

6. The Burbles

"Right, what's going on?" bellowed the Captain, as the Burbles buzzed round us like a swarm of excited bumblebees.

"The Jelloids have taken our Queen hostage!" cried Bopple.

"Why?" I asked.

"In case we try to stop them stealing the nectar from our lakes," said Bopple. "We are small, but we have nasty stings in our tails!"

"Why do the Jelloids want nectar?"

"As ammo for their gungerators – but nectar is our food!"

"The monsters!" I cried.

"That's just typical of the Jelloids," said Captain Thunderbolt.

"Can you save our Queen?" asked Bopple. "She is locked in a force-field bubble. We are no match for the Jelloids on our own."

"Have no fear, we'll put a stop to the Jelloids' nasty little games," declared the Space Patroller. "With all the gunge from your lakes, they could take over the universe! Can you show us where your Queen is being held, Bopple?"

"Of course," said the alien, anxiously. "But you will have to fight the Jelloids to get to her. We can help you, can't we, Burbles?"

"Y-y-yes," they stammered, looking very nervous.

"No, don't worry. That's what we are here for," said the Space Patroller. "Isn't that right, Alfie?"

"Oh, err, yes!" I spluttered.

Me? Fight the Jelloids? Oh, yikes!

7. Showdown!

Bopple, Jed and I squeezed onto the flying saucer with Captain Thunderbolt. Following Bopple's directions, we travelled up a spiralling tunnel and in no time had reached the surface of the planet.

Whoosh!

We zoomed across a bleak valley, skirted a petrified forest and soared over spiky mountains.

"Down there!" cried Bopple suddenly, and below us I spied the Jelloid's spaceship. It had an enormous hosepipe attached to its side, and was sucking up the goo from a nearby lake like a giant vacuum cleaner.

Jelloid guards were floating about like gruesome flying slugs.

Captain Thunderbolt landed the saucer behind a rocky ridge. We crept out silently, and crawled along the rough terrain like slithery snakes.

"There's our Queen!" cried Bopple, pointing with a long, thin finger.

The Queen was trapped inside an enormous bubble that hovered just above the ground. She was holding a golden sceptre and wore a tall crown and a flowing gown.

The Queen saw Bopple and waved
regally. She looked very pleased to
see him.

"Melting meteors!" I said. "How are we
going to break through the force-field?"

"Stand back," whispered Captain Thunderbolt. He took a fancy gizmo from his utility belt and aimed it at the bubble. "I'll soon have her out of there. Nothing can withstand the power of my Space Stunner."

He aimed and fired. *Kerpow!* A beam shot out, bounced back off the bubble and hit him in the tummy. His Stunner went spinning through the air as he landed in a heap on the ground.

"Oof," gasped the dazed hero, clutching his middle. "Nothing could penetrate that impenetrable orb, Alfie."

"Hang on," I said. I reached into my rucksack, took out the giant thorn I found on my last adventure, and jabbed it into the side of the force-field bubble.

This is the thorn I used to burst the force-field bubble. It's very, very sharp!

Bang! It burst like a balloon, and the Queen dropped to the ground. Then, raising her sceptre, she pointed over our shoulders.

"I think we have company," she said calmly.

I spun round to find four ugly Jelloids hovering in the air, their gungerators at the ready.

"Interfering fools," they said, gurgling like drains. "You pay for this."

Glop! A dollop of gunge shot from a gungerator and I dived to the ground as it spattered on the rocks behind me.

Splodge! Splat! Globules of gunk rained down, and we darted this way and that, trying to find cover.

"Ha! Ha! Gurgle, gurgle," sniggered the dribbling monsters. "Fun time over. We blast you into outer space."

Oh, yikes!

"Grrr!" growled Jed and he raced towards the Jelloids, barking and snarling.

"Come back, you'll be gunged!" I cried, but Jed wasn't listening. I gave a long, sharp blast on my dog whistle. Its thin peep split the air and the slimy Jelloids began to wriggle and writhe like eels.

"Waah!" they howled, screwing up their ugly, dribbling mugs.

Aha! I thought and blew the whistle again. *PEEEEP!* The Jelloids dropped their weapons and covered their ears. *PEEEEP!*

"Arrgh! It makes our brain ache!" they cried, and all around us the slimy green creatures began laying down their gungerators. "Please stop!" they begged.

"Only if the whole, horrible lot of you pack up and clear out," I ordered.

"Anything, just no more whistling, please!" they wailed.

My special dog whistle

8. The Teleporter

While Bopple escorted his Queen back to safety in their underground home, Captain Thunderbolt confiscated all the gungerators.

I rounded up the Jelloids and marched them onto their spaceship. If they tried any funny business, I gave a quick blast on the whistle and, clutching their ears, they became as meek as little lambs.

At last they were all aboard and, with a deep hum, the spaceship rose slowly into the sky.

"You haven't heard the last of us, Alfie Small," came a defiant, gurgling voice over the ship's loudspeaker.

"Oh, I'm shaking in my boots!" I yelled. "Now clear off, you overgrown jellybabies!"

"Yeah, clear off!" agreed Captain Thunderbolt, and with a sudden flash, the spaceship had gone. "Well done, Alfie," said the Captain. "Now let's go and see how the Burbles are doing."

We flew the flying saucer back below ground. The Burbles were waiting for us, and as we entered their dim cave they roared and cheered and clapped and hummed.

"Thank you, Alfie. Thank you, Jed, and thank you, Captain Thunderbolt!" cried Bopple.

"You saved our planet," said the Queen, waving her golden sceptre over our heads. "I appoint you all Heroes of Burbania."

"This is for you, your Majesty," I said with a bow, and handed her my dog whistle. "In case the Jelloids ever come back."

"Well, if we're handing out prizes, you'd better have one of these, Alfie," said the Captain, pinning a badge to my sweatshirt.

This is my Special Cadet badge

It's brilliant!

"You are now a Special Cadet in Space Patrol."

"Wow, thanks!" I said.

Just then, a delicious smell, from far, far away, drifted through the air. I lifted my nose and sniffed. "Mmm, my tea's ready," I said. "I need to get home, but my rocket is at the bottom of a lake!"

"No problem," buzzed Bopple. "Follow us."

In a far corner of the cave, Bopple and the Queen stood Jed and me in a small alcove in the rock. Two metal domes were lowered over our heads.

"This is our Intergalactic Transporter," said Bopple. "Just press that button, and wish where you'd like to go."

My hand hesitated above the button.

"It's perfectly safe," said the Queen.

Should I press it?

I pressed it, and the whole room began to hum. Jed and I started to turn invisible. I thought and thought of home.

"Bye Alfie. Bye Jed," called Captain Thunderbolt and the Burbles, as Jed and I disappeared completely.

Stars spun round us as we fell through darkness. Then – *Bump!* – we landed in a patch of springy grass, back to our old selves once more. Scrambling to my feet, I pushed through the tall and tangled weeds and came out from behind the shed at the bottom of my garden.

"Alfie, your tea is ready," I heard Mum call. "It's sausage and mash."

Mmmm, lovely – as long as we don't have jelly for afters!

"C'mon, Jed," I cried and we raced up the garden path.

I am Alfie Small, the famous explorer, and I can't wait for my next adventure to begin.